Emily watched out of the  mesmerized by the changing constantly white landscape below. Then something caught her eye – a patch of creamy yellow fur. It was moving fast, galloping over the snow. She peered closer – a tiny black nose and eyes, ears flattened in alarm. "It's a cub!" she gasped. "There's a polar bear cub below, all on its own!"

Meet all of Emily's

WILD FRIENDS

WWF 'WILD FRIENDS
PANDA PLAYTIME
THINK BEFORE EXTINCT!
CAN EMILY SAVE THE PANDA CUB'S FOREST HOME?

WWF 'WILD FRIENDS
TIGER TRICKS
THINK BEFORE EXTINCT!
CAN EMILY HELP THIS LITTLE TIGER FIND ITS MUM?

WWF 'WILD FRIENDS
POLAR BEAR WISH
THINK BEFORE EXTINCT!
CAN EMILY REUNITE SNOWY WITH HIS POLAR BEAR FAMILY?

WWF 'WILD FRIENDS
SNOW LEOPARD LOST
THINK BEFORE EXTINCT!
WILL LEO THE SNOW LEOPARD SAVE THE DAY?

WILD FRIENDS

POLAR BEAR WISH

By Linda Chapman and Michelle Misra

Illustrated by Rob McPhillips

RED FOX

WWF WILD FRIENDS: POLAR BEAR WISH

A RED FOX BOOK 978 1 849 41693 1

First Published in Great Britain by Red Fox,
an imprint of Random House Children's Publishers UK
A Random House Group Company

This edition published 2012

1 3 5 7 9 10 8 6 4 2

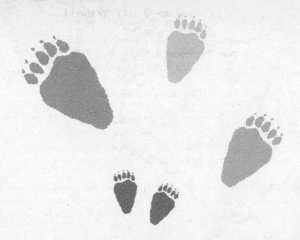

**Turn to page 77 for lots
of information on WWF,
plus some cool activities!**

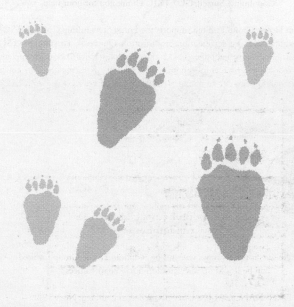

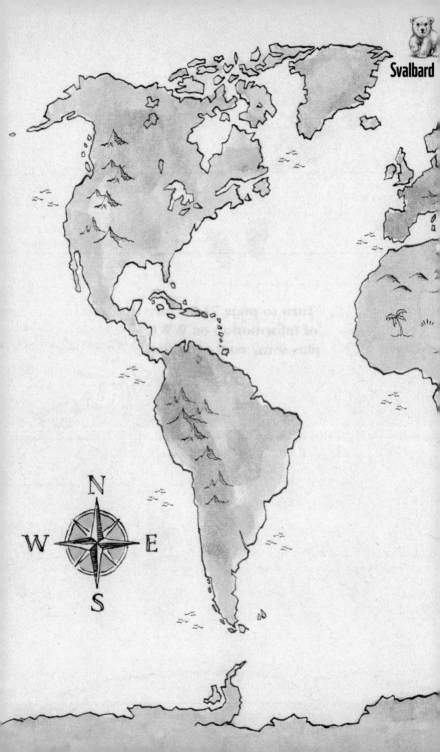

Svalbard

Diving In

The swimming pool echoed with the sound of happy shrieks and laughter. It was a weekend, so the pool was even more packed than normal.

"Here I go!" Emily Oliver said to her friend, Molly.

Emily put her hands above her head and dived in. As the water closed over her, every sound from outside was blocked as she whooshed down. *This must be what it's like to be a seal*, Emily thought. *Or a polar bear!*

Before she and Molly had gone to the

pool they'd been watching a documentary on polar bears and there had been some pictures of them swimming in the sea. Emily's parents worked for WWF, an organization that worked to protect wild animals and their habitats. Emily's mum was a photographer and in a few days' time she was travelling to the Arctic to take photographs of the polar bears that lived there. Emily and her dad were going along too. Emily couldn't wait!

She burst through the surface, shaking the water droplets from her dark hair.

"Good dive, Em!" her dad called from the side of the pool, where he was keeping an eye on Emily and Molly.

"It really was!" Molly agreed. Emily glowed. Molly was a great diver and her praise meant a lot.

"My turn!" Molly went on. She jumped high and dived in very neatly, her body

going straight down through the water.
"Touched the bottom!" she whooped as she surfaced.

"I've never been able to touch the bottom," said Emily enviously.

"You need to jump higher and get your body straighter," Molly explained. "My dad taught me to do it by putting his arm out so I had to jump over it when I dived in. Why don't I do that for you?"

"OK," Emily agreed eagerly.

Molly crouched on the side of the pool and put her arm up to about the height of Emily's knees. "Go on. Jump over my arm as you dive in."

Emily suddenly felt a bit uncertain.

Molly's arm looked very high.

"I'm not sure that looks too safe, girls," Mr Oliver said, coming over. "Maybe you should just stick to diving as you normally do, Em? You haven't been diving as long as Molly."

But Emily didn't like Molly being able to do stuff she couldn't. "I'll be fine, Dad," she said with more confidence than she felt. She counted to herself in her head. "One . . . two . . . three . . ." She bent

her knees and sprang into the air but she
was concentrating so hard on jumping up
over Molly's arm that she forgot to point
her body downwards properly. Her limbs

waved wildly and she belly-flopped into the
water.

OW! The thought filled her head as she
tumbled beneath the surface. Her tummy
really hurt from where it had smacked

down. She surfaced, coughing, her eyes streaming.

Her dad rushed over to the pool's edge, helping Emily up the steps out of the water. "Are you all right, sweetheart?"

"Yes, I'm fine, Dad," she gasped.

"Oh, Emily, I'm really sorry. That was my fault," Molly said anxiously. "That looked painful. Are you sure you're OK?"

"Yes," Emily insisted, not wanting to make a fuss. "And it wasn't your fault at all."

"Do you want to try again?" Molly said.

"Not right now," Emily said quickly. "Can we just swim for a bit? Maybe play tag?"

"Sure!" Molly jumped in and the two of them started playing. As Emily swam up and down, the soreness faded. After a while, Molly climbed out. "I'm going to do some more dives!"

Emily got out with her and looked at the rippling water. All she could think about was how much the last dive had hurt. *Come on, don't be a chicken*, she told herself. She stood on the side and raised her arms up by her ears but she felt sick. What if she belly-flopped again?

"Time to go now, girls!" Mr Oliver announced, and Emily breathed a sigh of relief.

"Can I do just one more dive?" Molly asked quickly.

"Alright then." Mr Oliver smiled. Molly climbed out and went to the deep end. "How about you, Em?" he asked.

Emily shook her head. "I don't want to."

Her dad frowned. "You know, if you've had a bad experience it's important to have another go and not let it put you off. Why don't you try again?"

"I haven't been put off," Emily said with a frown. "I just don't want to."

"Em, it's not like you to give up."

Emily felt tears sting her eyes. "I'm not giving up!" she protested. "I just don't want to dive any more today. I'm going to have a shower." She got out of the pool and hurried away to the changing rooms before her dad could stop her.

By the time Emily had showered and changed she felt better. She'd dive next time she went swimming. It was no big deal. She ran outside with Molly, her dad following them.

"Isn't it warm for the end of April?" Emily said.

Molly nodded. "I wish it could be this hot all the time!"

"It might be lovely for us," said her dad, "but remember that it's not such good news for animals that live in cold places."

"Why?" asked Molly.

Emily knew. "It's hotter because of global warming, and that's affecting animals who live in places like the Arctic – animals like polar bears."

Mr Oliver nodded. "That's right, Em. Polar bears need thick sea ice to hunt seals from. They're not normally fast enough to catch a seal swimming in the water so the way they get their dinner is to stalk seals on ice or wait at the seals' breathing holes and catch them as they come up to the surface," he explained. "As the climate is changing and the world is heating up, the ice is forming later in the winter and melting faster in the spring, so every year there is less time for the polar bears to hunt and feed."

"That's really bad because it's important that polar bears eat loads before summer arrives," Emily said. "They then live on their fat for the next four months or so when it's harder for them to catch seals because there's no sea ice. If the sea ice disappears earlier then the bears can't get fat enough to survive, and they starve." Emily knew lots about all kinds of animals, and she'd been reading up about polar bears especially ever since she'd found out about going to the Arctic.

"Poor things!" said Molly. "Are polar bears really rare then?"

"They're not as rare as animals like tigers or giant pandas," Mr Oliver told her. "There are still about twenty five thousand polar bears in the wild but the numbers are falling fast. If global warming continues to get

worse then some scientists
think that in thirty or
forty years there'll
be hardly any polar
bears left in the wild."

"But that would
be awful!" Molly looked
alarmed. "Can't something be done?"

"WWF are trying, aren't they, Dad?"
said Emily quickly.

Her dad nodded. "Yes, we're trying as
hard as we can to make people aware of
what's going on and persuade them to
become greener – recycling more, saving
on petrol and heating, being more careful
about how they use energy. It all helps to
reduce climate change. But people often
don't think that what they do on their own
at home has any impact. It really does
though. It's so frustrating. If only everyone
would do a little bit it would make such a

difference to the world – and to some of the beautiful creatures in it. Still, even though it sometimes feels like we're fighting a losing battle, we're not going to give up."

"We should write a story for the school newsletter," Molly said thoughtfully. She liked writing stories and articles. "We could put in some photos from your trip after you get back, Em. And tell people about how the polar bears are dying out."

Emily nodded. "That's a great idea. Let's do it!"

"We could start it tomorrow when you come round to my house," Molly said. She tucked her arm through

Emily's and grinned. "After we've
been swimming, of course!"

Emily forced herself to smile. Molly's
mum had promised to take them to the
swimming pool the next day too. *But I
don't want to dive*, Emily thought, feeling
scared. She took a breath. She would feel
differently in the morning, she was sure.

However, when Emily stood at the pool's
edge the next day she got butterflies in
her stomach and decided not to try. Molly
was too good a friend to tease her about
it or make her dive when she didn't want
to, and she seemed happy enough to just
play tag in the shallow end. Emily felt
bad though and was glad
when they left the pool
and went back to Molly's
house to write their story
for the school newsletter.

When Emily got home that afternoon she packed her suitcase and then got out one of her books on polar bears. She turned to her favourite picture – a mum lying on her side with two cubs cuddling up to her. As Emily turned the pages she heard a squeak coming from the large cage where her chinchilla, Cherry, lived. Cherry looked like a very large grey hamster, but with a curling fluffy tail and massive ears. She was sitting on a branch squeaking hopefully at Emily.

Emily smiled. "All right, you can come out."

She opened the cage door. Cherry
scampered into Emily's hands and gave a
squeak. Emily squeaked back. She loved
imitating the noises animal made. Putting
her head on one side, Cherry made a
chattering noise and Emily copied it.

She thought about polar bears. They
didn't make many sounds but she had heard

some cubs make a contented chuntering noise in one of the documentaries she'd watched. She tried it out. Cherry's ears twitched and she looked alarmed. Emily grinned. "Sorry, Cherry! I'll stick to chinchilla noises for now!"

As Emily cuddled her, she glanced at the polar bear picture again. Tomorrow she'd be going to the Arctic. Maybe she'd even see a real-life polar bear. She simply couldn't wait!

A Snowy Arrival

The Olivers flew to Oslo and then on to
a small airport called Longyearbyen in
the Svalbard islands of Norway. From
there they got a tiny plane to Ny-Ålesund,
a remote settlement where there were
a number of different research stations,
including the base that the WWF team
worked from. Staring out of the window as
the plane flew over the snow and ice, Emily
felt like she was arriving in another world.

There was a single row of seats on either
side of the aisle and Emily looked round
at the other passengers on board. Her dad

explained that most of the people who
went to Ny-Ålesund were researchers and
scientists, working on projects there – some
were studying and monitoring animals,
others were examining the land and climate
change. They came from all over the world
to do research.

Ny-Ålesund was just a small collection of
low red, blue and yellow buildings clustered

on a snowy peninsula with a frozen fjord
around it and snow covered mountains
behind. The air was clear and blue and the
snow sparkled in the sunlight. Around the
buildings the white wilderness stretched
out as far as the eye could see. It looked
just like a scene from a Christmas card.
Emily almost expected to see Santa and his
reindeer waiting for them in the snow!

The little plane bumped down and everyone zipped up their coats a little further before piling out of the plane. Emily was very glad of her cold weather gear – her big red coat and thick trousers, ski gloves and woolly hat. The air was so cold that it stung her cheeks. Emily thought of Molly back at home. She'd probably be in her T-shirt and shorts playing outside in the sun. But Emily wouldn't have traded places with her for anything!

The Olivers were met by a tall man with blond hair and a beard. "Welcome to Svalbard!" he said warmly, shaking Mr Oliver's hand. "My name is Arne. It's lovely to meet you face to face instead of just over

email. It'll be great to
get some photographs
of our polar bears,"
he added to
Mrs Oliver.

"Arne is
WWF's Polar Bear
Conservation
Co-ordinator here,"
Mrs Oliver told Emily.

"What do you have to do?" Emily asked
him curiously.

"I co-ordinate the team who are
monitoring the polar bear population," he
explained. "We record how many bears and
cubs there are, and in the spring and autumn
we try to measure them and monitor their
health. We also put GPS collars on as many
of the females as we can."

Emily nodded. She'd seen GPS collars
before, on a female panda she'd met in

China. She knew they sent radio signals to a satellite which then sent the information to a computer so that researchers could follow an animal – watching where it went and how far it travelled.

"The collars are really important," Arne said. "With the sea ice melting faster, we need to be able to see the effect it has on the bears – where they go to and what they do, how they feed and where they have their cubs. When we get to the base I'll be able to show you the bears we're tracking at the moment." He rubbed his gloved hands together. "Now, let's drop your luggage off at your apartment, and then we can head out for some food. You must be hungry after all your travelling."

"Well, we did have some food on the first plane," Mrs Oliver said.

Arne's eyes twinkled. "Ah, but now you are in Norway you will have some proper food – the best food in the world!"

He loaded their rucksacks into a truck. The roads were covered in snow and ice but the truck had snow tyres on and Arne drove them safely into the small town. He pointed at the tiny post office. "It's the most northerly post office in the whole world," he said.

Emily looked round. There were just a few people walking about between the buildings and a large wire pen, which held several barking huskies.

23

"There aren't many people here, are there? Is it always like this?" she asked.

"It's busier in the summer when the snow has melted," Arne replied. "More scientists come then, and there are also some tourists who visit on boats, but even in the summer it's still fairly quiet. Now, here we are." He stopped the car outside a dark red clapboard building with white window frames. "Your apartment." He took out some keys. "It's simple but it should have everything you need."

The apartment was on the second floor and the windows looked out onto the snow dunes. It had two small bedrooms and an open plan living area, and was simply decorated in blue and white.

The Olivers left their rucksacks there and then Arne drove them to the research station.

It had lots of windows and a roof platform with antennae on it. There were snow scooters parked outside. "Lots of different research teams use this station as their base," Arne explained as he led them inside. "There are five permanent members of staff who look after the computers and equipment. At the moment the WWF team are the only research team here though."

Just inside the door there was a lobby with several pairs of boots. Arne explained that in Norway it was considered polite to always leave your footwear by the door. They all took off their boots and hung up their outdoor gear, and then he took them to a meeting area with big windows where a man and a woman were sitting drinking coffee. They got up to shake hands with the Olivers.

"Hi, I'm Annika," said the woman, who had short blonde hair. "And this is Lars. We work for WWF. We're both polar bear biologists."

"It's great to meet you," said Mr Oliver, shaking hands. "I'm Mike Oliver and this is my wife, Heather, and daughter, Emily."

Lars was broad shouldered with a beard and glasses. "We've heard about your work around the world. It's great to have you both here – and you too of course, Emily," he added.

"This is such an amazing place!" Emily

said, looking out through the window at the vast expanse of white snow.

Annika smiled. "Just wait until you go out in one of the helicopters. Once you fly away from the settlement you will feel like the rest of the world doesn't exist."

"It's so bright here," said Emily's mum. "The light quality is incredible. I should be able to get some great photos."

"*If* we can find some polar bears for you," said Lars. "There have only been a couple of confirmed sightings so far this spring."

Arne nodded. "We know of eleven female bears with collars on who definitely came here to build maternity dens in November. Eleven is a lot less than we would hope for but the sea ice took a long time to form in the winter. Out of those eleven females we've no way of knowing if they or their cubs have survived the winter until they emerge and we pick up that they are moving from the GPS signals. So far, we've only seen three of the eleven moving."

"But there may also be some females we haven't collared," Annika said. "And we might see some male polar bears too – we don't collar the males."

"Why not?" asked Emily curiously.

"Their necks are wider than their heads and so the collars just slip off," said Annika with a smile.

"Now, please – sit down," said Arne. "I'll get some food organized. I went to the shop earlier. There's only one shop here in Ny-Ålesund but it supplies all we need."

Emily sat down and listened as the adults talked more about the weather conditions. She wondered what sort of food they

would have here. She could feel her tummy
rumbling. She hadn't eaten much since they
had set off that morning. *I hope I like it*, she
thought.

She needn't have worried. When Arne
came back in with a massive tray, the food
looked delicious! There were thick slices of
bread, pâté, cured salmon, pickles, tomatoes
and radishes. "Proper Norwegian food," he
said proudly. "Now, tuck in!"

Annika fetched some glasses and orange

juice to drink. Emily and her parents started to eat, making themselves open sandwiches by piling the bread high with the delicious toppings.

"Do you like it?" Arne asked Emily.

"Oh yes!" she said. The ham and cheese sandwiches her mum made her for lunch at school would seem very boring from now on!

As they were eating, two of the permanent members of staff came in and introduced themselves – Tim, the station manager, and Mary, a computer technician. They were very friendly and keen to hear about Mrs Oliver's plans to try to photograph the polar bears.

"When will we go out in the helicopter?" Emily asked.

"Tomorrow morning, first thing," Arne replied. "Fingers crossed we find some polar bears for you to photograph."

🐾 POLAR BEAR WISH 🐾

Emily nodded. Her fingers
and toes were *very* tightly
crossed. She went to the
window. The glass was cold
despite the warmth of the
building inside. She gazed across
the snowy landscape. *Oh, please let us see
some polar bears*, she prayed.

Looking for a Polar Bear

The whirring noise of the rotors filled the helicopter as Lars flew them over the snowy plains and glaciers. They were heading for Kongs Karl Land – five little islands which were very popular places for polar bear mums to make their maternity dens. Emily

looked out of the window while her mum
and dad chatted with Arne.

"Won't the polar bears be scared by the
helicopters?" Emily asked above the noise.

"In general, the bears don't seem that
bothered by helicopters," Arne replied.
"And we only use helicopters when we
absolutely have to. We certainly don't want
to contribute to global warming if we can
help it. A lot of the time we travel using snow
scooters or by cross-country skiing."

"I wonder if we'll see any cubs today,"
Mrs Oliver said. "It would great to get
some photos of them."

"It's a good day for it," said Arne. "Clear skies, not too cold – although the weather can change very rapidly here. If I was a mother bear it would be the sort of day I would choose for bringing my baby out of the den for the first time." Emily tried not to giggle. With his tall, broad-shouldered frame and shaggy mop of blond hair, she could almost imagine Arne as a polar bear!

"So, how long do the cubs stay here?" Mr Oliver asked.

"A couple of months maybe; it depends on the sea ice. As it starts to melt and break up the mothers tend to follow it, using every moment they can to hunt seals and eat before the ice goes completely. But now the ice is breaking up more quickly and melting faster we've found from our collars that the mums and cubs often have long swims between ice floes. Last year some of them swam for more than thirty miles without stopping."

"Thirty miles!" echoed Emily. "That's a long way!"

"Too long," Arne said seriously. "Half the cubs we tracked last year did not survive."

Emily swallowed. She hated the thought of the beautiful bears dying out in the wild.

They flew on in silence for a while until they reached the island of Kongsøya. There was an incredible feeling of stillness to the land. The only moving thing they saw was a flock of geese flying in the distance, their strong wings powering through the air as they flew across the blue sky.

Kongsøya was covered with big snow cliffs and drifts that looked like sparkly white sand dunes. "The polar bear mothers make dens in the drifts, don't they?" Mr Oliver said.

Arne nodded. "They stay in them all winter and then emerge about now, digging their way out. The mothers won't have eaten anything for up to six months, so they'll be very hungry." He checked a small hand-held device. He could use it to pick up the signals sent from the bears' collars when he was away from the computer – and it would also provide him with information about each bear. "There's a bear near here. Keep your eyes open, everyone."

Emily stared out at the white landscape. She was longing to see a polar bear.

"There!" Mrs Oliver said after a little while, pointing down.

"That's it! Bear N23991," Arne said, looking at his device. "Each bear has a number."

Emily saw the polar bear beneath them.

She was sitting very still on the ice, her creamy yellow fur standing out against the brilliant white of the snow. Emily was so excited she could hardly breathe. Her first wild polar bear sighting! "What's she doing?" she asked.

"Watching an *aglu*," Arne answered. "It's a hole a seal has made in the ice. Seals use them to come up and breathe. The polar bears sniff out the seals and then they sit and wait at the hole until a seal appears. They pull them out of the water by hooking them with their big front claws. They have to be very patient and wait a long time – sometimes days."

Emily looked at the majestic polar bear below them. She didn't seem bothered by the helicopter. It was hard to imagine how hungry she must be if she hadn't eaten for months. She was certainly completely focused on waiting for her meal.

Arne checked the information he had on the bear. "She's five years old. Annika and Lars spotted her emerging for the first time two days ago with a very small cub. It was noted as unusual because most polar bears have twins or triplets."

"Twins or triplets?" Emily was surprised. "Why's that?"

"It's just the way it is," her mum said. "Some large animals tend to have single babies – like horses and elephants. Others have twins or triplets."

"Most bears have two or three cubs," Mr Oliver said.

"Well, this polar bear has only one cub," said Arne. "Can anyone see it?"

They all peered through the helicopter's windows but there was no sign of a cub at all.

"Maybe she's left the cub in the den?" Emily suggested.

Arne shook his head. "Mother bears don't leave their cubs in dens. Usually the den is destroyed when they dig their way out." He looked grim. "This isn't good. If the cub isn't with his mum, something could have happened to him."

Emily bit her lip as she looked at the mother polar bear all alone on the ice. "Like what?"

"An adult male might have killed him. That sometimes happens. Or he could have just been too little to survive."

Mr Oliver squeezed Emily's arm. "These

things happen, Em. Try not to be upset. The mum will breed again and hopefully have more cubs next year."

The helicopter set off on its way. But as they flew on, Emily watched the lonely polar bear getting smaller and smaller in the distance. She couldn't stop herself from thinking about the little cub. She hoped that he was all right.

It was a long day, and they saw two more polar bears. Both were wearing radio

collars and had twin cubs with them. Mrs Oliver got some photographs of the mums and cubs together. Emily loved seeing the babies as they trotted beside their mums.

After a while Lars called round to them. "There's a

blizzard heading this way. We should return
to base." He guided the helicopter round
and they began to fly back towards the
research station. Mr and Mrs Oliver started
to look at the photographs on the camera
and Arne talked to Lars about where the
snowstorm was.

Emily watched out of the window,
mesmerized by the changing but constantly
white landscape below. Then something
caught her eye – a patch of creamy yellow
fur. It was moving fast, galloping over the
snow. She peered closer – a tiny black nose
and eyes, ears flattened in alarm. "It's a
cub!" she gasped. "There's
a polar bear cub below,
all on its own!"

The adults swung
round. By the time
they looked out
of the window the

helicopter had flown on past the cub.

"Where?" demanded Arne.

"Back there!" Emily exclaimed.

"But a cub wouldn't be out on its own," said her dad.

"I saw it! There *is* one! Please turn round," Emily begged.

Arne hesitated and then nodded and spoke to Lars. Lars manoeuvred the helicopter back round. But there was nothing below them.

"You must have imagined it," her mum said.

"I didn't!" Emily peered about desperately and suddenly caught sight of movement in a snowdrift below. "There!" she cried. "Look!"

A small cub was trying to dig a hole a little way up the drift. His paws scrabbled in the snow.

"Oh, my goodness. You're right, Em!" gasped Mrs Oliver. "It *is* a cub!"

Mr Oliver looked all around. "There's no sign of a mother bear anywhere though."

The helicopter flew down closer.

Emily's heart went out to the baby. He looked very small and alone in the snowy wilderness.

"Something must have happened to his mum," Arne said. "No mother would leave a cub that age. He can't be much more than three months old."

Lars checked the flight instruments
and looked back over his shoulder. "The
blizzard's getting closer!" he called. "We
haven't got much time."

Emily's heart thumped in her chest.
The cub couldn't be out on his own in
a snowstorm. He might not survive.

"We can't leave him!" she said. "We've got to do something!"

Beneath them the little cub dug even more frantically in the snow . . .

A New Friend

"We'll have to take the cub with us!" Arne decided. "There's a chance his mother has fallen ill and he's wandered away from his den and got lost. But we can't check the area now, not with a storm coming. If we leave him out here he may die."

Lars flew the helicopter down a little way off from the bear. Arne opened the door and jumped out. Mr and Mrs Oliver and Emily followed. The helicopter rotors whirled round above them. The cub was still digging part way up the drift, his small round ears pressed back against his head.

Arne crouched down at the bottom of the slope. "There now, little one. It's all right."

The cub looked round at the humans warily. Emily joined Arne and crouched down beside him. Arne reached out a hand but the cub shrank away and started scrabbling again as if he wanted to hide.

Emily remembered the noises she'd heard the polar bear cubs making in the documentaries she had watched at home. She made an attempt to imitate the chuntering noise. The cub looked round.

She made the noise again. "*Ch . . . ch . . . ch . . .*" The cub hesitated and then he took a cautious step towards her.

Arne shifted backwards. "Well done. Keep going," he breathed.

Emily felt the world shrink to just her and the cub. All she focused on was the baby polar bear. "*Ch . . . ch . . . ch . . .*" She made the noise again. The cub scented the air, as if sniffing her. He obviously decided he liked the smell, as he padded a few paces down the slope. But then his paws lost their grip. His legs slid apart and he landed on his tummy, sliding down the slope straight towards Emily!

She didn't have time to do anything.
He bumped right into her and her arms
closed protectively around him as she fell
backwards into the snow. She heard her
parents and Arne gasp. Blinking, she looked
up. Her arms were full of cub and he was
staring down at her in surprise with his
bright black eyes. "Hello," Emily said softly.

The cub snuffled curiously at her face.
She sat up, not wanting to scare him. But
now he was in her arms he seemed very
happy.

Emily looked round at
her parents. Her mum
was clicking madly
with her camera. Her
dad looked like he
couldn't believe it.
"Well, well. It looks like
once again you've made
a new friend, Em!"

Arne helped Emily to stand up with the cub in her arms.

"Can you manage to carry him into the helicopter?" Arne asked.

Emily nodded. He wasn't that heavy and she could sense from the way he was cuddling into her that he liked being held.

"*Ch . . . ch . . . ch . . .*" she whispered into his fur and he licked her cheek.

"If he panics I'll take him," said Arne. "But while he's happy with you, let's stick with you getting him into the helicopter."

Emily climbed back inside and sat down with the cub. He looked around the helicopter inquisitively.

They rose into the air. The cub tensed but Emily stroked and soothed him and he gradually relaxed.

As they flew away, Arne and Emily's mum and dad looked closely for any signs of an adult polar bear but the icy landscape was deserted.

"No sign of his mum anywhere," said Mr Oliver.

Mrs Oliver smiled at Emily. "I bet you didn't think you'd be cuddling a polar bear, Em!"

"No!" Her eyes glowed. It was amazing. "What's going to happen to him?" she asked anxiously.

"We'll get him back to the base and check him out. Then, when the weather settles, we'll come back here and look for his mum. I've noted down where we found him so we can see if there are any females nearby. His mother may be unwell. If she is then we might still be able to help her and reunite them, but if he's an orphan we'll have to send him to a zoo."

"A zoo!" Emily cried.

"I know, it isn't ideal." Arne sighed. "But there isn't really anything else we can do."

"Couldn't another polar bear foster him?" Emily asked. "One who's lost her own cub?" She knew that certain animals would sometimes foster babies who weren't their own. She thought about the bear they had seen out on the ice earlier that day – the bear without a cub.

Arne smiled sadly. "Ah, I can see where you're going with this, Emily, but I'm afraid not. It's almost unheard of for polar bears to foster other cubs. An adult who wasn't his mother would probably just chase him off. In the worst case, she might kill him."

Emily hugged the cub even more closely. She didn't like

to think about him having to live in a zoo all his life but it would be a million times better than being killed. She buried her face in the cub's thick fur. *Please let your mum still be alive, and let us find her,* she thought.

Feeding Time!

Emily held the bottle of milk and the cub
sucked hungrily at the teat. It reminded her
of a time she had fed a baby lamb back in
England! Arne and Annika had checked the
polar bear over, weighing and measuring
him and taking small samples of blood
and hair. They had made up the bottle of
milk and shown Emily how to feed him.
Then they'd gone off with Emily's dad to
check the position of all the bears that were
wearing GPS collars, while Emily carried
on feeding the cub and her mum took
photos.

The cub was hungry but the examination had shown that he was healthy and well-nourished. It appeared that he hadn't been without his mum for long.

"Come on, Snowy, drink up," said Emily, tilting the bottle more so the cub could get at the last drops.

"Snowy?" her mum said, raising an eyebrow.

"Arne said I could think of a name for him," Emily said. "Do you like Snowy?"

"I think it's a perfect name for him." Mrs Oliver smiled and ruffled the cub's fluffy cream coat.

The little cub sucked the last few drops of milk and then started to investigate the room. There were low windows with window ledges. Snowy walked along

sniffing them, and then put his front paws up on a ledge and pushed at the glass with his black nose. Dropping down, he started to explore some more. His paws seemed too large for his body and he walked clumsily. He sniffed in every corner, and then came over to where Emily was sitting on the floor and snuffled at her hair. As she stroked him, Snowy flopped down and rolled onto his side like a dog. She tickled his white tummy and he pawed at the air, sticking his tiny black tongue out.

Emily giggled. "That's not very polite!" she teased him.

"We should get him something to play with," said Mrs Oliver. "Bears like to investigate things. Wait here."

She returned a few moments later with a large cardboard box and a football, her camera around her neck. "Here, let's see what he does."

She put the box and the ball on the floor. Immediately Snowy got up and went over to check them out. He walked around the ball. As he knocked against it, it rolled. He stared in surprise and then followed the ball,

pushing it with his nose. Emily giggled as he dribbled the ball around until it reached a corner and got stuck.

Losing interest, Snowy headed over to the box. He sniffed it all over and stuck his head inside the gap at the top. Then he tried to climb on top of it, his front legs and tummy clutching it, his back legs scrabbling to get up.

Emily and her mum both laughed as he slid off, landing in a heap in the straw.

"Oh, Snowy!" Emily went over and hugged him. "You're so cute!" He climbed onto her knee and snuggled against her. Emily pulled her arms around him and kissed his head. She stroked his back and felt his breathing change as he fell asleep.

"One very happy cub," said Mrs Oliver.

"Yes, but he'll be even happier if we can find his mum," said Emily. She was torn. She wanted to cuddle Snowy but she also wanted to go and see if Arne and Annika had found out anything about his mother.

Mrs Oliver seemed to understand. "I'll go and see if there's any news. You stay here for a while and enjoy playing with him. You might never get a chance to be this close to a polar bear ever again. Make the most of it!"

Emily smiled and cuddled Snowy as her mum left the room. She was planning on making the most of every moment!

A little while later, Emily's mum came back with Arne. Snowy's eyes flickered as he heard them come in but then they shut again and he went back to sleep.

"Well?" Emily asked.

"It may be good news, it may not," said Arne, crouching down to stroke the cub. "There's a collared bear near to where we found Snowy. She could be his mother."

"Is she in a den or is she moving about?" Emily asked.

"She's moving. In fact, you've seen her before. It's the bear that we saw hunting for seals."

Hope leaped through Emily. "The bear who had lost a cub! But when we saw her earlier she wasn't anywhere near him. Could Snowy be her cub?"

"He's certainly about the size of the cub she was spotted with a few days ago," Arne said. "What we can't work out is why he was on his own and why they were so far apart. He and his mum might have got separated if a male polar bear had come along, I suppose, or there is a slight chance he could have wandered off to explore while his mother was waiting at the seal hole. Most cubs his age wouldn't do that, but an exceptionally bold and curious cub might."

"Snowy's really inquisitive," Emily said. "He was looking all round this room." She stroked Snowy's fur and then frowned. "But wouldn't his mother have noticed if he'd gone off?"

"Remember that she probably hadn't eaten for six months," Mrs Oliver said. "She'd have been pretty fixated on catching some food."

Emily thought back to the female polar bear on the ice. She had barely even flickered an ear at the helicopter overhead. Perhaps Snowy did belong to her and had wandered off without her knowing?

"If she is his mum, she'll probably have tried to follow his scent," Arne said.

"So she'll be wandering around looking

for him," said Emily in dismay. Her arms tightened around the cub as she thought about his poor mother wondering where he was.

"As soon as the weather improves we'll take him back," Arne said glancing outside to where the blizzard was still raging. "We'll use the tracker to locate her."

"And then they can be reunited," said Emily in relief.

"If she *is* his mother – but remember we don't know that for sure," said Mrs Oliver. "Snowy may have a different mother. There's still a chance his mum could be dead or injured."

"So, how will we know if the bear with the collar is his mum?" Emily asked.

"There's nothing for it but to watch how they react when they first see each other," Arne explained.

Emily swallowed, remembering what he'd

said about polar bears killing little ones if they weren't their own. "But if he isn't her cub, she might attack him."

Mrs Oliver squeezed her shoulder. "I know. It will be risky but Arne will take a tranquillizer gun. If it looks like Snowy is in danger, Arne will put the adult bear to sleep and we'll be able to get Snowy away."

Emily nodded but she couldn't help feeling worried. She imagined Snowy cowering as a full-grown adult tried to attack him. He'd be terrified. And what if the tranquillizer dart missed, and the bear wasn't put to sleep in time? She swallowed. It was a risk – but one they were simply going to have to take.

A Brave Move

At this time of year there was almost no night-time in Ny-Ålesund – it was dark for just a couple of hours. Emily woke up early and pulled back the thick blackout curtains that kept out the daylight. The morning sky was blue and there was no wind. She stifled a yawn as she pulled on her warm clothes. She'd been so worried about Snowy that she hadn't slept well, despite feeling worn out by everything that had happened the day before.

After a quick breakfast of bread, cheese, salami and tomatoes they went to the base. Emily fed Snowy his morning bottle of milk and then Arne said they could take the little cub to try and find his mum. Snowy seemed happy for Emily to carry him back onto the helicopter. She held him tightly as they flew towards the island.

"The GPS signal says the bear we're looking for has travelled to the edge of the island," said Arne. "She must have gone there to hunt." He broke off. "There she is!"

Emily caught her breath as she saw the large cream-coloured polar bear. She was standing on a floating chunk of ice,

separated from the rest by a strip of dark blue water. "How will we get Snowy to her?" she said.

"We'll have to land and get him out of the helicopter," said Arne. "If Snowy is her cub, hopefully when she sees him she'll recognize him and swim over. We can watch from the safety of the helicopter."

Lars brought the helicopter down to land but kept the rotors whirring in case they needed to make a quick get-away. There was no way of knowing what the female polar bear would do. If she decided to confront them it could be very dangerous. Polar bears rarely attacked humans, but they could certainly kill one if they wanted to.

Arne helped Emily out. Her mum and dad followed and then Arne fetched the tranquillizer gun, just in case. Emily glanced at her parents. Their faces were tense. Her mum had her camera at the ready.

The female had noticed them as they
arrived but then turned her back, focusing
on the water around her again. Her long
shaggy coat rippled as she moved.

Emily followed Arne away from the
helicopter. Snowy stiffened in her arms as
he spotted the other bear, and started to
struggle. The female still had her back to
him.

"Put him down; let's see what happens,"
Arne said.

Emily gently put the
cub onto the ground.
As she bent over he
started to struggle
and jumped out of
her arms. He began
to lollop towards the edge
of the ice, his paws slipping in all directions.

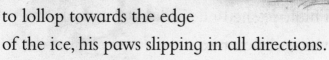

"It looks as though he might recognize

her," Emily said, filling with hope.

"Or is it just because she's an adult polar bear and he thinks it's his mum?" said Arne.

Emily felt her stomach flip. What if Snowy had got it wrong and the bear wasn't his mum? The little polar bear stopped at the edge of the ice and paced up and down anxiously. He dipped a paw in the water and stopped himself.

"He won't have learned to swim yet," said Arne. "We need her to turn round and see him."

Snowy put his other paw into the water and then jumped back.
It was clear that
he was scared of
it. Opening his
mouth, he made
a high-pitched
whimpering noise.
The female bear

lifted her head and swung round, looking over her shoulder. Snowy stepped closer and made the noise again.

Emily held her breath as the adult bear's dark eyes fixed on the little cub. What would she do?

Then the female lumbered round and stared across the water, her head low, her nostrils flaring. Snowy suddenly seemed to throw his fear to one side and jumped into the water! It engulfed his small white body, his head just poking up out of it as he paddled frantically towards the adult bear.

"Oh, Snowy!" Emily's hands flew to her mouth. What would happen?

The female bounded into the water to join the little cub. Emily's heart felt like it

had stopped in her chest. She watched as
in three swift seconds the female reached
Snowy. Her jaws opened wide for a moment,
and then she plunged her head down into
the water.

"No!" gasped Emily.

"It's all right," Arne said quickly. "Don't
worry. Watch!"

Emily watched through the fingers of her
gloves as the huge polar bear shoved her
nose under the cub and started helping him

through the water. She pushed him up
onto the ice and clambered out herself.
Snowy gambolled around her, his fur wet
but his eyes shining. He reached up to her
with his nose.

"It *is* his mum!" Emily said in delight.

Arne nodded, smiling warmly.

The mother bear reached out and
cuffed Snowy with one big paw, rolling
him over and over in the snow. He
crouched down, uncertain.

"That's her telling him off for running
away!" said Arne.

With one bound, the mother reached
him and flopped down in the snow beside
him. The cub crawled up to her on his
tummy. She moved onto her side and he
cuddled up against her. She put one large
paw around him, pulling him in close and
licking his head with her black tongue, a
look of utter happiness on her face.

"And that's her telling him she loves him," said Mrs Oliver softly.

Emily swallowed, happy tears prickling her eyes. Snowy was back with his mother. Arne squeezed her arm. "Let's leave them in peace," he said.

Emily nodded and followed him back to the helicopter. As she reached the step, her dad put his arm around her shoulder. "If you hadn't spotted Snowy, the world might have one less polar bear in it now," he said.

Mrs Oliver nodded. "Well done, love."

Emily looked back at the happy polar bears. She knew what her parents had said was true but she was sad to be leaving him behind, knowing she would never see him again. "Bye, Snowy," she whispered.

"You know," Arne said as Emily climbed back into the helicopter, "there's

Take a look at some of the pictures that inspired this story

Polar bear (Ursus maritimus), Two fighting Churchill, Canada. October 92 ECO: 118 Image No: 27369 © François Pierrel / WWF-Canon

Two adult males fight it out!

This polar bear contemplates an icy dip!

Polar bear (Ursus maritimus) standing on the edge of an ice flow. Spitsbergen, Svalbard, Norway. 01.01.2008 Image No: 226489

Seeing daylight for the first time is a magical moment for this cub.

Looks like this bear has been rubbing his nose in it!

A female Polar bear (Ursus maritimus) emerging from her maternity den near Churchill, Manitoba, Canada. Image No. 229340 © David Jenkins / trackerbaz.com / WWF-Canada.

Polar bears can measure up to three metres tall when standing on their hind legs.

Two cubs cuddle up to their mum.

This mother's cubs are nearly grown up – but they still like to stay close!

Look at the size of this bear's paws!

a rule here. Anyone who helps a polar bear gets to come and see how that polar bear is doing the following year. Would you like that?"

Emily grinned at him. "That's not really a rule, is it?"

"It is now," Arne chuckled. "As I'm head of the research team, I'm making it one! We'll be able to keep an eye on Snowy by tracking his mum. He'll stay with her for at least another eighteen months. So, next year, you could come back and see him."

Emily looked at her mum and dad, who nodded. "That would be great!" she grinned.

The helicopter's rotors whizzed faster and it rose up into the air. Beneath them the mother bear crouched down in the snow, and Snowy clambered up onto her back. He clung on with his front and back paws, his tummy snuggled against her fur.

The mother bear seemed to smile and then padded off contentedly across the snow.

⋆

Three weeks later Emily was back in England, and her adventure in the Arctic seemed like a distant dream. The moment she had got home, she'd stuck a picture of Snowy onto the giant map on the wall in her bedroom. She loved looking at that picture, and wondering what Snowy was up to. Arne had been in touch to let

her know that they'd seen Snowy several
times since he'd been reunited with his
mum, and he was growing bigger and
more confident every day.

"So, are you going to dive in then?"
Emily's daydream was broken by her
dad, who was sitting by the swimming
pool, smiling at Emily as she stood at the
water's edge.

Emily gazed at the rippling pool.
Butterflies flapped in her tummy as she
thought about diving in, but then she

thought about another stretch of water thousands of miles away – and a brave cub who had been afraid, but hadn't let that stop him.

"Yes," she smiled at her dad. "I am." And bending her knees, she dived smoothly into the turquoise water.

Read on for lots of amazing polar bear facts, fun puzzles and more about WWF

WWF

Polar Bear Fact File

Best feature: Their thick, fluffy coat which keeps them warm in the Arctic.

Size: Polar bears are the world's largest land mammal, and an adult male polar bear usually measures about 2–3 metres high and can weigh up to 680kg. That's about ten times the weight of the average human!

Favourite food: Polar bears like to eat seals, although less than 2% of their hunts are successful. They can smell seals under one metre of snow and from almost a kilometre away!

Home: Polar bears live in the frozen Arctic, near coasts, on islands or on the sea ice itself. They are found in Greenland, Norway, northern Canada, Alaska and Russia.

Current population: There are approximately 20,000-25,000 polar bears living in the wild today, with 60% of the population of wild polar bears living in Canada.

Breeding and family: In the wild, a pregnant polar bear will dig a deep snow den to prepare for the cubs' arrival. Most mothers give birth to twins but they can have up to three cubs. The mother will spend two months in the den before welcoming the babies, who live with her in the snow drift for another four months, absorbing their mother's body heat and milk. After this, they are able to leave the den, but stay close to their mother for about 2 years. The cubs do not need a father figure: in fact, polar bear couples are only together for a week before they separate – that's a quick romance!

Life span: A polar bear's average life span in the wild is 15–18 years, but polar bears in captivity can live until their mid to late 30s.

Biggest threat: The biggest threat to polar bears is climate change. The sea ice is melting earlier than before, making it harder for the polar bear to survive without food during the lean seasons.

Bonus fact: Polar bears are excellent swimmers. In fact, their Latin name (Ursus maritimus) means 'Sea Bear' – an apt name for this amazing species which spends much of its life in, around, or on the water.

Polar Bear Crossword Quiz

See if you can find the answers to this crossword
quiz below ... It tests you on the story and fun facts!

ACROSS

3 At the beginning of the book, Emly is swimming with her friend _ _ _ _ _ (5)

4 Emily's chinchilla is called _ _ _ _ _ _ (6)

5 Polar bear mothers usually give birth to _ _ _ _ _ (5)

7 Emily feeds the cub a bottle of _ _ _ _ (4)

9 To track the polar bears, WWF put GPS _ _ _ _ _ _ _ on them (7)

DOWN

1 The country the Olivers visited was _ _ _ _ _ _ (6)

2 Polar bears most often live in the _ _ _ _ _ _ (6)

6 Polar bears like to eat _ _ _ _ _ (5)

8 Emily gives the cub a _ _ _ _ to play with (4)

10 The cub Emily discovers is called _ _ _ _ _ (5)

Across: 3. Molly 4. Cherry 5. Twins 7. Milk 9. Collars
Down: 1. Norway 2. Arctic 6. Seals 8. Ball 10. Snowy

W☉rd Scramble

The names of these characters from
the book are all jumbled up.
Can you unscramble them?

LLYMO

☐☐☐☐☐

RNEA

☐☐☐☐

MELYI

☐☐☐☐☐

KAINAN

☐☐☐☐☐☐

RO MILREV

☐☐ ☐☐☐☐☐☐

Cub Alert!

Oh dear, Snowy is on his own again!
Can you lead him through
the maze to his mother
on the mainland?

START

FINISH

Spot the Difference

Can you spot the five differences
between these two polar bear pictures?

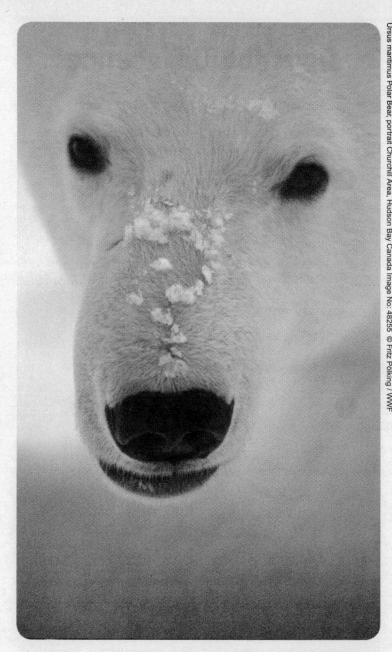

More about WWF

WWF

You're probably familiar with WWF's panda logo, but did you know that WWF . . .

- 🐾 Is the world's leading conservation organization.

- 🐾 Was set up in 1961 (when TV was still black and white!).

- 🐾 Works with lots of different people around the world, including governments, businesses and individuals, to make a difference to the world we live in.

- 🐾 Is a charity and most of their money comes from members and supporters.

WWF's aim

The planet is our most precious resource and we need to take care of it! WWF want to build a future where people live in harmony with nature.

WWF are working towards this by:

🐾 Protecting the natural world.

🐾 Helping to limit climate change and find ways to help people deal with the impacts of it.

🐾 Helping to change the way we live, so that the world's natural resources (like water and trees) are used more carefully, so they last for future generations.

A female Polar bear (Ursus maritimus) with her two young cubs, in the snow, near Churchill, Manitoba, Canada. Image No: 229495
© David Jenkins / trackerbaz.com / WWF-Canada

What do WWF do?

* **Conservation** – Protect rare species of wild animals
  and plants as well as important ecosystems found
  in forests, rivers and seas.

* **Climate change** – They don't just tackle the causes of
  global warming, but also the impacts of climate
  change on communities and environments.

* **Sustainability** – Help to change the way we all live,
  particularly in richer developed countries like the
  UK, including decisions about what we eat, buy
  and use for fuel.

How can I help WWF?

There are lots of ways you can take action in your own home to help protect our beautiful planet and the people and animals that live on it. Here are a few ideas to get you started . . .

Buy sustainable

One of the biggest threats to a lot of wildlife, including the giant panda, is loss of habitat. This is often from people cutting down trees to use in paper or wood products, or to make way for roads, and clearing areas to use for farming.

You can help stop this by only buying products that are sustainably farmed, or wood and paper products from sustainable forests.

So when you're out shopping with your mum or dad, look for:

- **Certified paper and wood products** (look for the FSC logo to tell if something is certified or not)

- **Products made from certified sustainable palm oil** (look for the RSPO logo to be sure that they are certified)

If your local shops don't stock these products – ask them why!

Reduce, reuse, recycle!

Households in the UK send 18 million tonnes of rubbish to landfill yearly. That's more than any other country in Europe!

Top five tips to reduce waste

Why don't you do some of these over a week and see how much less rubbish you throw away than normal?

Take a reuseable bag when you go to the shops, instead of picking up a new one.

Take any clothes, shoes, books or toys you don't want any more to a charity shop.

Clean out old food jars and pots to use for storage.

Get creative with your rubbish and make a kitchen-roll penguin.

Make postcards by cutting old birthday and Christmas cards in half, and give them to your friends.

"Go Wild!"

The way we live can affect people, wildlife and habitats all around the world. Making small but important changes to the way we act really can help to save polar bears in the Arctic or orang-utans in Borneo and Sumatra.

And this is what the Go Wild club is all about. It's your chance to learn more about some of the animals and habitats that we're working to protect. It's also about discovering what you can do in your own home to help look after the natural world.

By joining WWF's Go Wild club at *wwf.org.uk/gowildjoin*, you will recieve a member's pack and magazines that will take you on an incredible journey around the world, meeting some amazing animals and individuals. You'll find out what life's like for them and the threats they face to their environments.

As well as getting lots of Go Wild goodies, being a member means that you help WWF to continue their work. Join today and explore your wild side!

Don't miss Emily's adventure with cheeky
snow leopard cub, Leo, in the next
Wild Friends adventure . . .

Read on for a sneak peek!

A New Adventure Begins

Pale green eyes, light grey fur covered
with darker spots, a cat-shaped face . . .
Emily Oliver studied the picture of the
majestic snow leopard in her book. She
loved all animals but there was something
particularly beautiful about snow leopards
with their magical eyes and white-and-grey
fur. Ignoring the usual school playground
noise around her, she wondered what it
would be like to meet a real snow leopard.

I might be about to find out, she thought
excitedly. On Saturday, she and her mum
were flying to the Altai Mountains in

Mongolia where snow leopards lived.

Emily's mum and dad both worked for
WWF. It was an organization that helped
protect endangered animals. Her mum was
a photographer and her dad worked on
different projects all around the world. He
had flown to Mongolia a month ago to help
set up a new snow leopard project. He wasn't
going to be back until Christmas – a whole
two months away. Emily had been really
missing him but at least she was going to
spend half term with him.

Emily shut her book. Usually she played
with her best friend, Molly, at lunchtime but
now Molly had got one of the main parts in
the school Christmas play and was rehearsing
most lunchtimes. It was strange not having
her to hang around with. The two of them
had been best friends since they were little.

I'll be glad when the play's over, Emily
thought with a sigh.

The bell rang and Emily lined up with the other children from her class. When she got into her classroom she found Molly there already, sitting on a desk talking to Jade who was also in the school play.

"Hi, Emily!" Molly called.

"Emily!" Jade whooped. She was always very loud and Emily felt a little bit shy around her.

"What have you got there?" Jade demanded, pointing to the book as Emily went over.

"A book," Emily replied.

"Duh!" Jade rolled her eyes. "Really? I thought it was a *dog*!" She  spluttered with laughter as if she'd said the funniest thing in the world, and snatched the book from her. "What's it about then? Hey, it's a white lion!" she said, seeing the picture of a snow leopard on the front.

"It's not a lion," Emily told her. "It's a snow leopard."

"Lion? Leopard? Same thing," said Jade, shrugging. "Animals are boring."

"No, they're not!" Emily protested.

"Whatever." Jade grinned. She gave
Emily the book back and turned
her back on her. "Hey,
Molls, do you remember
in rehearsal just now . . .
dingbat!" She pulled a
funny face.

Molly giggled. "Yeah, I
thought I'd never stop laughing."

"Why? What happened?" asked Emily
curiously.

"It was just something in rehearsal that
Ethan did," said Jade. "You wouldn't get it."

Molly nodded. "You probably had to be
there, Em."

"*Dingbat*!" Jade said again and they both
laughed.

"I'm . . . I'm going to put my book
away." Emily hoped Molly would come
with her but Molly stayed with Jade.

"So, can you come to my house at half term so we can practise our lines?" Emily heard Jade say to Molly.

"Yeah. That would be fun," Molly replied.

Emily felt a stab of jealousy. Molly was *her* best friend. For a moment, she almost wished she wasn't going to Mongolia. What if Molly decided she liked Jade more than her while she was away? She glanced back and saw Molly and Jade laughing together again.

Feeling like a balloon that has just been pricked by a pin, Emily sat down at her desk.

"How's the packing going then?" Emily's mum bustled into Emily's room later that evening. Her long red hair was caught up in a messy bun.

"It's not really," sighed Emily. She was lying on her bed thinking about Molly.

"Come on, there's no time for lazing around!" her mum said in surprise. "We need to get packed tonight. It's an early start to the airport on Saturday and we've got lots to do tomorrow. Now, have you packed some T-shirts and fleeces?" she asked, checking the rucksack lying in the middle of Emily's floor.

"Yeah," said Emily quietly.

"And warm pjs and your dressing gown?"
Emily nodded.

Mrs Oliver frowned. "Are you all right,
Em?" she asked.

Emily shrugged. "Yep."

But her mum wasn't
fooled. "OK, come on,
what's the matter?
I thought you were
looking forward to
going to Mongolia."

"I am! It's just . . ."
Emily swallowed and
then the words burst
out of her, "It's Molly!"

"Molly?" Her mum
looked surprised. "What's the matter
with her?"

"Nothing's the matter. But she's been
rehearsing loads with Jade and they're
going to practise together all over half-

term . . ." Emily wondered if her mum would understand.

"Oh, I see," Mrs Oliver said slowly. "You're worried that Molly will want to be friends with Jade more than she wants to be friends with you?"

Emily nodded miserably.

"Oh, Em. You and Molly have been best friends since you were four. I'm sure Molly isn't going to suddenly want to change that. It's natural that she wants to spend time with Jade if they're both in the play and she probably does want to be friends with her – but not best friends like she is with you."

Emily fiddled with the ends of her dark hair. "But what about when I'm not here, Mum?"

Her mum squeezed her shoulder. "If she's a real best friend it won't matter whether you're here or on the moon, she'll still want to be your best friend. It's like with Dad. Just because he's away, it doesn't make us love him any less, does it? Now, come on" – her eyes held Emily's – "you know I'm right."

"I guess," said Emily, feeling a bit better.

"You must stop worrying." Her mum smiled. "We have an adventure to go on and snow leopards to see!"